This book belongs to

....

Happiness

Wisdom

Cocoa

Beauty Sleep

This is the story of Crystal Clean,

the sleeping daughter of a king and queen.

On every page, can you guess what?

There's a feather duster for you to spot.

This edition first published in 2010 by Castle Street Press
an imprint of make believe ideas ltd.

Copyright © 2007 make believe ideas ltd.
27 Castle Street, Berkhamsted, Hertfordshire, HP4 2DW, UK.
565, Royal Parkway, Nashville, TN 37214, USA.

Sleeping Beauty

Illustrations by Sara Baker

Once upon a time,
a king and queen
hold a big party.

They are very happy
because they have a baby girl.
Her name is Crystal Clean.

Seven good fairies
give presents
to the baby princess.

Mary
Rose

Mary
Lou

Charm

Happiness

9

Then a bad fairy comes.
Her name is Griselda.

"The princess will prick her finger on a needle," says Griselda. "She will die!"

"No," cries the youngest fairy.
"The princess will not die.
She will sleep for a hundred years."

Every day, the queen
tells Crystal Clean,
"You must never touch a needle!"

But one day, the princess
finds a secret room.

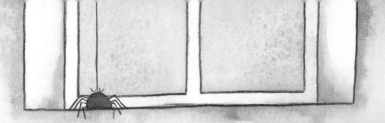

She sees a spinning wheel.
The princess pricks her
finger and falls down.

DO NOT TOUCH

Everybody falls sound asleep.
They sleep and sleep
for a hundred years.

One day, a prince
finds the castle.

21

He kisses the princess,
and she wakes up!

The prince marries the princess. Everyone has a big party!

Ready to tell

Oh no! Some of the pictures from this story have been mixed up! Can you retell the story and point to each picture in the correct order?

Picture dictionary

Encourage your child to read these words from the story and gradually develop his or her basic vocabulary.

castle

fairy

needle

party

presents

pricks

prince

princess

spinning wheel

Key words

Here are some key words used in context. Help your child to use other words from the border in simple sentences.

The king **and** queen have a baby girl.

She will prick her finger.

A prince finds the castle.

He kisses **the** princess.

They hold a big party.

a • he • is • said • go • you • are • this • going • they • away • play • cat • to

the • dog • big • my • mom • no • dad • all

Make a spinning star

You might not have a spinning wheel at home, but you can still weave a colorful woolen star. It's so simple!

You will need

2 sticks of equal length, such as chopsticks or toothpicks • lengths of wool in different colors

What to do

1 Form a cross with the sticks, then use the wool to tie them together, finishing with a knot. Do not cut the wool
2 Keeping the wool taut, weave it under and around each stick in turn. The circle will gradually get bigger as you work toward the end of the sticks.
3 Change colors every so often by tying in a new strand of wool whenever you feel like it.
4 Experiment with weaving the wool in and out in different ways.
5 If, when you have finished, you have any gaps, try weaving in lengths of ribbon. You can also try making little shapes out of cardboard or wood and gluing them onto your woolen star.
6 To hang up your star, tie a length of wool through the woven wool at the top of one stick, make a loop, and knot it. Pin up your star and let it spin!